My Working Mom

by Peter Glassman

illustrated by Tedd Arnold

HarperCollins *Publishers*

For Sandra Glassman,
my very own working mom
—P.G.

For D.R.M.
—T.A.

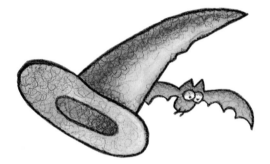

Watercolors and colored pencils were used for the full-color artwork.
The text type is 23.75-point Galliard.

My Working Mom
Text copyright © 1994 by Peter Glassman
Illustrations copyright © 1994 by Tedd Arnold
Printed in Singapore. All rights reserved.

Library of Congress Cataloging-in-Publication Data
Glassman, Peter J.   My working Mom / by Peter Glassman ; illustrated by Tedd Arnold.   p.   cm.
Summary: Although she sometimes resents her mother's work as a witch, a young girl decides to keep her mother just the
way she is.   ISBN 0-688-12259-0 (trade) — ISBN 0-688-12260-4 (lib. bdg.) — ISBN 0-06-441033-1 (pbk.)
[1. Working mothers—Fiction.   2. Mothers and daughters—Fiction.   3. Witches—Fiction.]   I. Arnold, Tedd, ill.
II. Title.   PZ7.G481438My   1994   [E]—dc20   93-22036   CIP   AC

Visit us on the World Wide Web!
www.harperchildrens.com

It isn't easy having a working mom.

Especially when she
enjoys her work.

If Mom isn't busy in her lab,
she's flying off to a meeting somewhere.

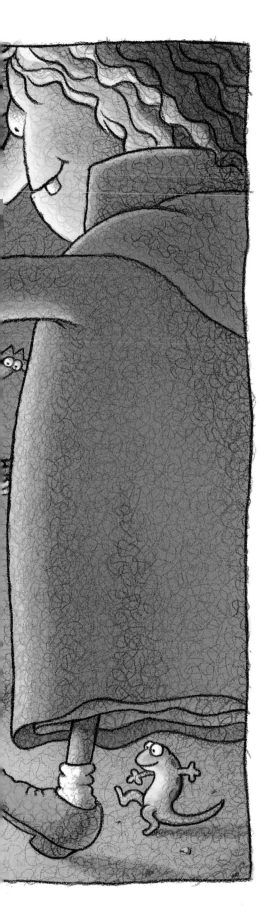

Mom says her
meetings are boring,
but I'll bet they're a blast!

Of course, sometimes Mom's work doesn't go quite the way she planned.

And when Mom's had a bad day at work—
watch out!

Sometimes I think Mom likes her job more than being a mom, especially when she makes one of her weird dinners.

Or yells at me for playing
with something she's working on.

Still, Mom always gives me the greatest birthday parties. And she never forgets to make me a cake that is out of this world!

If I'm in the school play,
I can count on Mom to be there—
even if she does usually arrive
at the last moment.

And when my team is playing,
no one cheers louder than Mom!

One day my teacher asked our parents to come to school and talk about their jobs.

Some of the parents were sort of dull,
a few were kind of creepy.

But not *my* mom!
All the kids thought
she was great!

Even though I don't always
like having a working mom,
I just can't picture mine
any other way.

So I guess if I had to choose,
I'd keep my mom just the way she is.